Nim and the War Effort

MILLY LEE ◆ Pictures by YANGSOOK CHOI

A SUNBURST BOOK ◆ FARRAR, STRAUS AND GIROUX

Nim covered the big round table with newspapers and carefully smoothed them. Then she set out nine pairs of chopsticks, nine bowls, nine plates, and six serving spoons. She looked across the room to see Grandmother embroidering a small satin slipper and Grandfather reading a Chinese newspaper.

"Grandfather, when you finish your newspaper, may I have it? Tomorrow is the last day of the paper drive."

Grandfather nodded, continuing to read.

Nim placed his shot glass and his bottle of Ng Ka Py on the table at the place of honor. "Grandfather, did I tell you about the policeman?"

Grandfather looked up from his newspaper. "What policeman?"

"Officer Kearny. He came to our class today to tell us about his work. He said that any time we needed help we could call the police on the telephone. Grandfather, do you think you could come to school sometime to tell about your work at the bank?"

"We'll see," said Grandfather, "by and by." He started to read again, nodding absently from time to time as Nim chattered on about the policeman's visit.

Nim's mother placed a large, steaming bowl of soup in the middle of the table and called the family to dinner.

Grandmother put down her embroidery and teetered on her small, bound feet as Nim helped her to her seat next to Grandfather.

When her grandparents were seated, Nim and her sisters and brother sat down. Nim asked everyone to be extra careful not to spill on the newspapers because she needed every piece for the paper drive.

Mother spooned out the soup, giving the first bowls to Grandfather and Grandmother before serving the rest of the family.

Then, as was done at every meal, Ed, the oldest child, invited everyone to eat. "*Sek fahn*, Grandfather. *Sek fahn*, Grandmother. *Sek fahn*, Mother." Nim and her sisters followed, in order of their birth, inviting their elders to "eat rice," in Cantonese. Finally, Grandfather picked up his spoon and began to eat. The others quickly followed. Mealtimes were quiet times; only the adults spoke.

When dinner was over and the table was cleared, Nim had eight more pieces of newspaper to add to her pile.

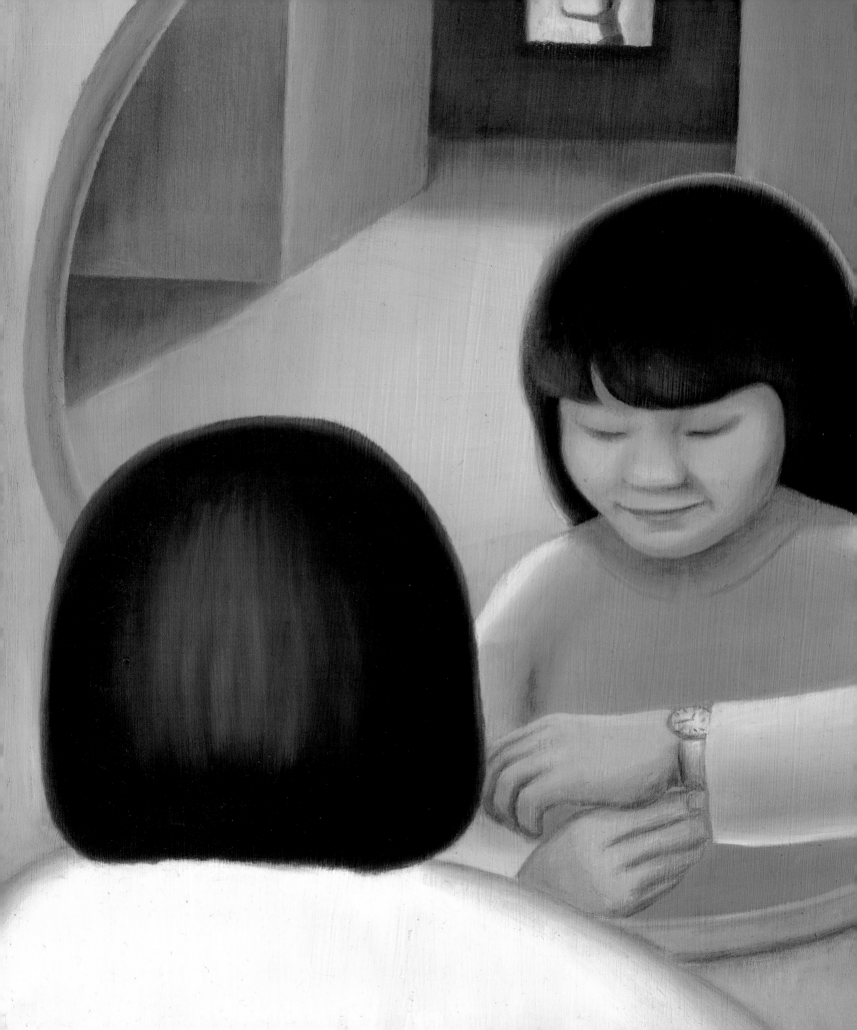

The next morning, Nim dressed quickly. She brushed her thick straight black hair and put on the gold watch Uncle George had given her. She decided to wear it for good luck, even though it was broken. Grandfather had punched another hole in the watchband, so it fit her perfectly now.

In front of the open window in the hallway, Grandfather was performing Tai Chi, starting the last set of slow, deliberate movements. Not wanting to disturb him, Nim went quietly to a breakfast of hot steamed rice with an egg and oyster sauce. Grandfather came into the dining room just as she finished eating.

"Good morning, Grandfather," Nim called cheerfully.

"You're up early today," said Grandfather. He was already dressed in his crisp white shirt, knotted black tie, a three-piece business suit, and polished black shoes. On the lapel of his coat was a small pin with two flags—the American flag and the Chinese flag. Many Chinese men began wearing the pin with two flags after the war with Japan started so they would not be mistaken for the enemy.

"Your Aunt Nell called last night," said Grandfather. "She's leaving some newspapers for you in front of her flat; they have your name on them and will be tied with red string."

"Good," said Nim. "Every bit helps. What time is it, Grandfather? Exactly."

Grandfather pulled out his pocket watch by its gold chain from his vest pocket. "It's six forty-seven. Exactly."

Nim whirled around the hands of her watch to set it. "That gives me just about an hour to collect papers before school starts?"

"An hour and thirteen minutes," said Grandfather. "And don't be late for school."

Nim smiled shyly at Grandfather. "May I collect a few more papers after school? The contest is over at five o'clock . . . and it's a tight race between Garland Stephenson and me. Our stacks are almost equal."

Grandfather listened and nodded yes. "But you must be home no later than three-thirty, so you can have your snack and get ready to go to Chinese school."

Nim went over to the cabinet in the dining room and picked up the cigar box she used for her Chinese-school supplies. "See, Grandfather, I have my brushes, ink box, and books all ready." She looked hopefully at Grandfather. "How about four o'clock?"

Grandfather hesitated. "Homework done?" he asked.

"All done; here is my calligraphy lesson."

"Three forty-five, then," said Grandfather gruffly.

Nim smiled broadly. "Thank you, Grandfather. I'll be home on time."

Grandfather helped Nim carry her rickety red wagon down the stairs to the sidewalk. She loaded a small bundle of newspapers and her schoolbooks onto the wagon and started up Sacramento Street. The wagon made creaking noises as she pulled it along. At the corner, Nim could see two large bundles of morning newspapers waiting for Mr. Wong, the newspaper vendor. She looked at them longingly.

Two doors away, Mr. Kwan, the butcher, was opening his shop for the day. *"Ho mai seen sahng!*—Good sales, sir," Nim called to him in Cantonese.

The butcher nodded as Nim stopped in front of his store. "Sorry," he said. "I can't give you any more newspapers, I need them to wrap meat."

Nim made a sad face, poking out her lower lip.

"Oh, all right," said the butcher. "Here are a few more papers for you, but that's all."

"Thank you, Mr. Kwan." Nim put the papers on top of her stack in the wagon. "Garland Stephenson is going to win the prize, but that's okay," said Nim, "because we'll all be helping in the war effort. It really doesn't matter who wins . . ."

The butcher threw up his hands. "What do I say to my customers? Put the meat in your pocket and carry it home because all the newspapers are needed for the war effort? All right, all right," he grumbled, handing Nim a few more papers. "But no more! And tell your grandfather I have some fresh oxtails for him. He likes oxtail soup, I know."

Nim thanked the butcher and looked at her watch. "What time is it?" She followed his eyes as he looked over to the clock on the far wall. Next to it was a large photograph of Mr. Kwan's son George in an Air Force uniform.

"Seven o'clock," he replied.

Nim adjusted her watch and waved goodbye. She headed up the block to her aunt's flat. But where were the newspapers tied with red string? Nim frowned. Maybe Aunt Nell had forgotten to put them out. Nim stood there for a moment, trying to decide whether to ring the doorbell so early in the morning or to come back after school.

Then she looked down the street and saw Garland Stephenson just disappearing around the corner, pulling a brand-new Radio Flyer wagon full of newspapers. On top of the pile was a large stack tied with red string.

Nim set off after him. Garland Stephenson might be twice her size, but he was not going to get her newspapers!

Garland had stopped in front of Mr. Wong's stall, which was still boarded up. He looked around to see if anyone was watching and then picked up the two big bundles of morning newspapers. They were heavy and unwieldy, and Garland had trouble putting them in his wagon. When he heard the creaking of Nim's wagon, he took off his gabardine jacket and quickly tried to cover the load.

"Those are today's papers," said Nim.

"What's it to you, Miss Know-It-All?" said Garland.

"You can't take them. They belong to Mr. Wong."

"Well, they're mine now," said Garland. "Mr. Wong shouldn't have left them lying on the sidewalk." Then Garland made a fist to threaten Nim. "And you better keep your mouth shut."

Struggling with his heavy load, Garland pulled his wagon down Sacramento Street.

Nim followed him, keeping her distance. "And where did you get the papers tied with red string?" she called. "You know my aunt left those for me!"

Garland mimicked her in a high shrill voice: "And where did you get the papers tied with red string?" He made a face at Nim.

The front wheels of the wagon jammed as he turned the corner. Garland tried to keep it from swerving, but the wagon fell on its side with a crash, spilling newspapers all over the sidewalk. The wagon wheels spun in the air.

"Keep away, stay back, these are mine!" Garland yelled frantically as he tried to catch the swirling papers.

Nim had to cover her mouth and bite her cheeks to keep from laughing. Garland looked like a scarecrow waving his arms and stomping his feet in the middle of a whirlwind of papers. Serves him right, she thought as she pulled her wagon past him.

"I've got news for you . . . you little runt," Garland yelled after her. "This is an American war . . . and it's going to be an American who wins the contest . . . not some Chinese smarty-pants."

Nim turned around to give him a cool, disdainful look. "Drop dead!" she said.

From a window above them, Nim's grandfather observed the scene.

School was out. Nim and her friends Vinny and Dorothy stopped by the auditorium to check on the height of the piles of newspapers stacked against the walls of the hall. Each stack was labeled with a student's name and classroom number. Some of the stacks towered over all the others—Nim's and Garland's—and they were right next to each other.

Nim had already decided what she must do to win. She would go outside of Chinatown to get more papers.

Nim leaned close to Dorothy. "Listen, Dorothy," she whispered. "Why don't we go all the way up to the big apartment houses on Nob Hill where the rich folks live? They must have tons of newspapers!" She looked slyly at Dorothy. "Do you want to go with me?"

"All the way up there?" Dorothy asked. "No, not me, my mother would find out. You shouldn't go up there either, Nim."

"How about you, Vinny?"

"No, I have an accordion lesson." Vinny backed away, visibly alarmed at the daring suggestion.

"Well, I guess I'll have to go by myself," said Nim.

As Nim left the school yard, she headed in the opposite direction from home. Nob Hill was six blocks out of her way. She would have to hurry to get there and back before three forty-five, as she had promised Grandfather. Nim's wagon seemed to squeak louder than usual as she pulled it up the hills along the quiet streets. There was none of the familiar noise and bustle of Chinatown here.

When she reached the top of the hill, Nim saw a white flag with a gold star displayed in a ground-floor window. She knew that the star meant the family who lived there had lost someone in the war. She decided it was a good place to start. An older man in a doorman's uniform was wrestling with a large steamer trunk outside the front door.

Nim approached him. "Excuse me," she said in a brave voice. "My school is having a paper drive to help the war effort. Do the people who live in your building have any newspapers to contribute?"

The doorman looked down at her and smiled. "Aren't you a little out of your territory?" he asked.

"Yes, but all the papers in Chinatown have been taken already," said Nim.

"Hmmmm . . . All the papers?" asked the doorman.

"Well, not all . . . but I came up here . . ." said Nim, pausing to think of what to say next.

"Well, good for you to work so hard for the war effort," said the doorman. "I have two grandsons in the service." He reached into the pocket of his jacket and took out a worn envelope. Inside were photos of two soldiers in uniform. He showed them to Nim.

"Where are they now?" asked Nim.

"In the Pacific," said the doorman, as he put the pictures away. "Well, then . . . newspapers! Step right this way!" He walked slowly to the garage, taking out a large ring with lots of keys, attached to a long chain. Nim followed with her wagon and watched as he unlocked the door. He entered and turned on the lights. Nim waited outside on the sidewalk. "Don't be shy," he said. "They're all yours!"

Nim looked past him into the garage. There, piled high from floor to ceiling, filling almost the entire garage, were stacks and stacks of newspapers. Nim was speechless. She had never seen so many newspapers in one place; there were more even than all the newspapers collected in the school auditorium.

"I've been meaning to borrow a truck to take them to the collection center," said the doorman.

"May I have *all* of them?" asked Nim.

The doorman smiled. "Help yourself."

Nim became thoughtful. She frowned and asked, "What time is it?"

The doorman looked at his wristwatch. "It's about twenty past three."

"Exactly?" asked Nim.

The doorman looked again. "It's exactly three twenty-three, and time for me to get that steamer trunk out of the doorway before someone bumps into it. You go ahead and take all the papers you want."

Nim adjusted her watch, and the doorman started to leave.

"May I use the telephone?" asked Nim.

"Help yourself," said the doorman. "It's on the table in the lobby."

The doorman returned to the trunk and Nim went into the building.

A few minutes later, a police car and a paddy wagon screeched to a stop in front of the building. Nim was waiting on the sidewalk outside the open garage.

A police officer jumped out of the car. "Who called for help?" he asked.

"I did. Please hurry," said Nim as she led him to the entrance of the garage.

"What's the problem?" asked the police officer.

"We need to get all these newspapers to Washington Irving School right away."

"We need to *what?*" exclaimed the police officer.

"Hurry, we need to get the newspapers to the school before five o'clock. What time is it now?" asked Nim breathlessly.

"Let me get this straight," said the officer. "You called the police here to move newspapers?"

The other policeman stared at Nim. "Why would you call the police?"

"It's for the war effort!" Nim said excitedly. "When Officer Kearny came to our school, he said if we ever needed help we should call the police. He said to give them the exact address and—"

"Wait a minute," interrupted the officer, shaking his head. "I don't think this is the kind of help Officer Kearny had in mind."

The doorman reappeared. "Is there a problem here?"

Nim explained, "I needed help with the newspapers, so I called the police. Does anyone know what time it is?"

Back in Nim's flat, the clock on the wall chimed three forty-five. Grandfather was pacing the floor nervously. On the table was Nim's snack of milk and cookies, and beside it was the cigar box with her Chinese-school supplies. Grandfather flipped through Nim's calligraphy book, as if checking her work.

The telephone rang. Grandfather answered it immediately. Nim's mother listened with a worried look. Grandfather thanked the caller brusquely and hung up. The phone rang again. Grandfather answered it; again he thanked the caller. When the phone rang a third time, Grandfather motioned to Nim's mother not to answer it. "Let it ring," he told her. Grandfather paced back and forth with hands clasped behind his back. Nim's mother could see that Grandfather was mad, but she didn't dare ask why. Soon Grandfather put on his hat and coat and left the house.

Outside the Washington Irving School, the police officers were just getting into the police car and the paddy wagon. Nim rushed out to wave goodbye, shouting, "Thank you, thank you for helping me."

It was late; Nim hurried home, pulling her empty wagon. She almost ran into Garland Stephenson, making his last trip before the end of the contest. His wagon was overloaded and he had to steady it as he pulled it slowly toward the auditorium door.

With a self-satisfied grin, Garland said, "Did you bring any more newspapers? As if you could ever beat me!"

Nim smiled mysteriously and said, "A few."

"Did you see how big my stacks are?" asked Garland.

"I saw them," answered Nim. "What time is it?"

"It's too late for you," said Garland. "And, by the way, why don't you get a watch that works? It would tell you it's time for me to win the contest," he added with a laugh.

Nim watched from the corner and chuckled as Garland opened the auditorium door.

Nim raced up the street with the empty wagon clattering behind her. She knew she was late, but she knew all would be forgiven when she told about winning the newspaper drive.

Grandfather was waiting in front of the house. Nim ran happily up to him, ready to share her good fortune. But she saw that Grandfather was very angry.

"You were seen riding in a police paddy wagon through Chinatown. You are late coming home. You have worried your mother and grandmother," he said sternly.

Nim nodded, her head lowered. She didn't say anything.

Grandfather continued: "I heard you and that boy fighting over the newspapers this morning. I heard what he said about winning."

Nim looked up at him, quietly protesting. "But I won."

"Winning isn't everything," Grandfather replied. "You have shamed our family. You have brought disgrace on all of us, and on our ancestors, just to prove that boy wrong."

Nim bowed her head again, totally dejected.

Grandfather continued: "Go upstairs, sit and reflect on what you have done. I will speak with you again after you have thought about it."

Nim climbed the stairs slowly. Mother opened the door. Nim nodded to her with tears in her eyes. Still, neither Mother nor Grandmother dared ask why Grandfather was so mad at her.

Nim walked slowly to the room the family used as their Ancestral Hall. She seated herself on the first of six straight high-back chairs arranged in a row against the wall on one side of the room. Above the chairs hung six large portraits of ancestors. They all looked austere and dignified. None smiled.

Nim sat very quietly by herself. She was too embarrassed and ashamed to meet the eyes of the Honorable Ancestors, who must be looking down at her in disappointment. The chair was very hard. The only sound in the room came from the ticking of the clock, and the chimes that rang every quarter hour. It was four-thirty now.

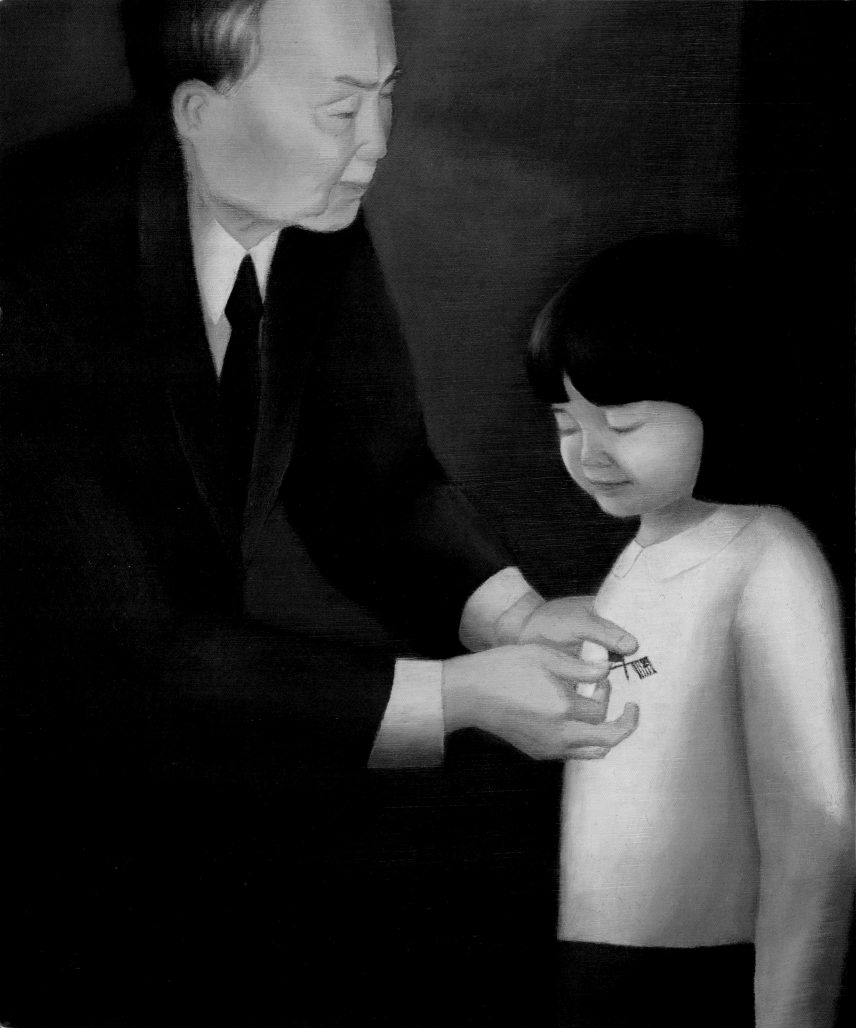

On the windowsill at the far end of the room were Grandfather's prized jade plants, glistening in the late-afternoon sun. At the other end of the room, close to the door, stood the family's ancestral altar. As he did every day at sunset, Grandfather came to attend the small altar. Without looking at Nim, he lit the incense from the flame on the wick in a small glass bowl filled with temple oil. The statue of Kwan Yin, the Goddess of Mercy, in its teak and glass case, was slowly enveloped in smoke. The sweet, pungent smell of incense filled the air as Grandfather murmured a short incantation. Then he turned to Nim.

She rose to face him. "Grandfather, I am sorry. I did not mean to shame the family. But I didn't do what I did to prove Garland wrong. I wanted to bring honor to the family. Garland said an American would win the contest, and he was right. An American did win. I was born here. I am the American who won."

Grandfather looked thoughtfully at Nim.

She was crying quietly, her head bowed.

Grandfather reached for the pin with the American flag and the Chinese flag that he wore on his lapel. He took it off and pinned it on Nim.

She looked up slowly, touching the pin lightly.

Grandfather handed her his handkerchief. "Come along now. If we hurry, we can stop by the school to see the newspapers before you have to go to Chinese school." He put on his hat.

Nim made a quick trip to the dining room to get her Chinese-school box. As she took a big gulp of milk and picked up her cookies, she looked at the newspaper on the sideboard. "Grandfather, are you finished with this?" she asked. "We need it for the war effort, you know."

Grandfather sighed. He really wasn't done with it, but he picked it up and tucked it under his arm. As they left the house, Nim shyly took Grandfather's hand.

Along the way, she told him about the newspapers in the garage and the help from the policeman. But, as much as she wanted to, she didn't tell him how exciting it was to ride through Chinatown in the police paddy wagon.

When they got to the school, they stood in the auditorium doorway to look at all the newspapers stacked against the walls and the piles of papers with her name on them filling the middle of the auditorium.

Grandfather handed the newspaper to Nim. "Be gracious in your moment of triumph," he instructed.

Taking the newspaper, Nim walked to Garland's stacks. She stood on tiptoe and reached up and placed it on top of one of the piles. Deliberately, she smoothed and squared it before she looked over her shoulder and flashed Grandfather an impish smile.

Grandfather looked pleased. "Now we must hurry if you are to be on time for Chinese school, my American grandchild."

For David, Linda, Peter, and especially for Kearn, with love —M.L.

For Lian Hua —Y.C.

Text copyright © 1997 by Milly Lee
Pictures copyright © 1997 by Yangsook Choi
All rights reserved
Distributed in Canada by Douglas & McIntyre Ltd.
Printed in July 2011 in Singapore by Tien Wah Press (Pte) Ltd.
First edition, 1997
Sunburst edition, 2002
5   7   9   10   8   6

Library of Congress Cataloging-in-Publication Data

Lee, Milly.
  Nim and the war effort / Milly Lee ; pictures by Yangsook Choi.— 1st ed.
    p.   cm.
  Summary: In her determination to prove that an American can win the contest for the war
effort, Nim does something which leaves her Chinese grandfather both bewildered and proud.
  ISBN: 978-0-374-45506-4 (pbk.)
  1. World War, 1939–1945—United States—Juvenile fiction.   2. Chinese Americans—Juvenile
fiction.   [1. World War, 1939–1945—United States—Fiction.   2. Chinese Americans—Fiction.
3. Competition (Psychology)—Fiction.   4. Grandfathers—Fiction.]   I. Choi, Yangsook, ill.
II. Title.

PZ7.L51433 Ni 1997
[Fic]—dc20

96-11595